Graphic design and illustrations: Zapp
Story adaptation: Robyn Bryant

© 1994 Tormont Publications Inc.
  338 Saint Antoine St. East
  Montreal, Canada   H2Y 1A3
  Tel. (514) 954-1441
  Fax (514) 954-5086

ISBN 2-89429-508-1

Printed in Hong Kong
Bound in China

THE FROG PRINCE

TORMONT

Once upon a time, there lived a princess who adored objects made of gold. Her favorite was a golden ball.

On hot days, she liked to sit beside an old well in the cool forest, tossing the ball in the air.

One day, the ball slipped from her fingers into the well, which was so deep that the princess could not see the bottom.

"Oh dear! I'll never find it!" the princess said, and began to cry.

Suddenly, a voice called out, "What's the matter, Princess?" When the princess looked around, she saw a green frog poking its head out of the water.

"Oh, it's only you," she said. "Well, if you must know, I'm upset because my golden ball fell into the well."

"I could get it back for you," the frog said. "But what will you give me as a reward?"

"Whatever you like, frog. What about my pearls and jewels," she suggested. "Or perhaps my golden crown?"

"What would I do with a crown?" the frog said.

"But I'll get your ball if you promise I can be your best friend, and come for dinner and sleep over at your house."

"All right," the princess agreed. But secretly, she thought the frog was talking a lot of nonsense.

The frog dove deep into the well, and soon returned with the golden ball in its mouth.

But as soon as he dropped it at the princess's feet, she grabbed it and ran home, without even a thank you.

"Wait!" called the frog. "I can't run that fast." But she paid no attention to him.

The princess forgot all about the frog, but the next day, as she was eating dinner with her family, she heard something come crawling *splish-splash* up the marble steps of the castle.

Then a voice called, "Princess, open the door!"

The curious princess ran to open it, but when she saw the frog standing there, all green and dripping, she slammed the door in his face.

14

The king could tell that something was the matter. "Has a giant come to get you?" he asked.

"Oh no, father. It's only an ugly frog," she said.

"And what does a frog want with you?" the king asked.

As the princess explained, they heard more knocking. "Let me in, princess," the frog pleaded. "Have you forgotten what you promised down by the well's cool water?"

16

"If you made a promise, daughter, you must keep it. Let him in," the king said.

With a long face, the princess opened the door. The frog followed her to the table, and said, "Lift me up beside you."

"Don't be ridiculous," the princess said, but her father gave her such a look that she changed her mind.

But the chair wasn't high enough, so the frog asked to be lifted onto the table. And once there, he said, "Push your golden plate closer so I can share your dinner."

The princess moved her plate, but it was quite clear she didn't enjoy the rest of her meal.

Once the frog had eaten his fill, he said, "I'm tired. Carry me upstairs so I can sleep in your room."

The thought of sharing her
room with the cold damp
frog so upset the princess
that she began to cry again.
But the king said,
"Get going. It's not
right to turn your
back on someone
who helped you
when you were
in trouble."

"Yes, father," the princess said, and carefully picked up the frog with two fingers. When she got to her room, she set the frog down in the corner farthest from her bed.

But soon she heard the frog plop down beside her. "I'm tired too," the frog said. "Lift me into bed, or I'll tell your father."

So the princess tucked him into bed, with his little green head resting on a fluffy pillow.

But when she got back into her bed, she was surprised to hear the frog sobbing quietly. "What's the matter now, little frog?" she asked.

"All I ever wanted was a friend," the frog replied. "But it's clear you don't like me at all! I might as well go back to the well."

At this, the princess felt very badly indeed.

She sat on the edge of the frog's bed. "I'll be your friend," the princess said, and this time she meant it. Then the princess gave him a goodnight kiss on his small green cheek.

Instantly, the frog transformed into a very handsome young prince. The princess could not have been more surprised and pleased.

Of course, the prince and princess became very good friends indeed.

And a few years later, they were married, and lived happily ever after.